This dragon book belongs to:

....

Teach Your Dragon Empathy
My Dragon Books - Volume 24
Written by Steve Herman

Copyright © 2019 by Digital Golden Solutions LLC.
Published by DG Books Publishing, an imprint of Digital Golden Solutions LLC.

ISBN: 978-1948040754 (paperback)
ISBN: 978-1948040761 (hardcover)

www.MyDragonBooks.com

First Edition: February 2019
10 9 8 7 6 5 4 3 2 1

Teach Your Dragon Empathy

My Dragon Books - Volume 24

When Diggory was a little guy,
he needed to be taught...
About the way he should behave
and ways that he should not.

At Diggory's school, Miss Nancy
keeps the lunchroom clean and neat;
She wipes the tables, mops the floor,
and we all think she's sweet.

Once Diggory spilled a glass of milk and then just walked away;

He did not pause to clean it up but went outside to play.

"Just get another pet," he scoffed.
"It's not that big a deal!"
Diggory did not even think
of how his friend must feel.

Ping Chang can't speak English well;
his family is Chinese.
When Diggory Doo first met him,
he began to laugh and tease.

Diggory Doo plays checkers;
in fact, he's really pretty good,
But when he won, he'd brag
and didn't act like winners should.

He made fun of his opponent
when the game was done;
And didn't notice that his friend
wasn't having fun.

When Diggory Doo was younger,
he refused to share his toys;
He only cared about himself,
not other girls and boys.

"Diggory Doo," I said,
"it's time to learn a brand new word;
I kind of have a feeling,
it's a word you've never heard."

Diggory scratched his head and said,
"What could this new word be?"
"I'm glad you asked me!" I replied.

"*Empathy* is a skill
which I highly recommend –
It's like a game of make-believe,
because you can pretend..."

"Imagine that you're someone else
instead of being you
To help you be careful
of the things you say and do."

I KNOW HOW YOU FEEL ...

"That after she has tidied up, you make a brand new mess."

"Think of how Miss Nancy feels! It's not kind, you must confess!"

"You would have been much kinder to your friend who lost her pet - You would have shared her feelings and helped her search, I bet."

Diggory said, "I think I see what *empathy* can do! It shows me that how others feel is how I would feel, too!"

We all should show some *empathy*
and be like Diggory Doo;
If Diggory Doo can learn it,
then you can learn it, too!

Read more about Drew and Diggory Doo!

POTTY TRAIN YOUR DRAGON
Steve Herman

TRAIN YOUR ANGRY DRAGON
Steve Herman

THE MINDFUL DRAGON
Steve Herman

THE YOGA DRAGON
Steve Herman

DRAGON & THE BULLY
Steve Herman

HAPPY BIRTHDAY DRAGON
Steve Herman

TRAIN YOUR DRAGON TO ACCEPT NO
Steve Herman

I GOT THIS!
Steve Herman

TRAIN YOUR DRAGON TO BE KIND
Steve Herman

A DRAGON With His Mouth ON FIRE
Steve Herman

TRAIN YOUR DRAGON To Follow RULES
Steve Herman

TRAIN YOUR DRAGON To Be RESPONSIBLE
Steve Herman

TRAIN YOUR DRAGON To LOVE HIMSELF
Steve Herman

TEACH YOUR DRAGON To Understand CONSEQUENCES
Steve Herman

TEACH YOUR DRAGON TO STOP LYING
Steve Herman

TEACH YOUR DRAGON TO MAKE FRIENDS
Steve Herman

Visit
www.MyDragonBooks.com
for more!